MW01045122

Krypton Ight

The First Steps of Adventure

Kelly Dopp

authorHOUSE®

AuthorHouse™
1663 Liberty Drive, Suite 200
Bloomington, IN 47403
www.authorhouse.com
Phone: 1-800-839-8640

First published by AuthorHouse 9/30/2008

ISBN: 978-1-4389-0455-9 (sc)

Printed in the United States of America
Bloomington, Indiana

This book is printed on acid-free paper.

Prologue

For sixteen years, Krypton Ight had been living his life the simple way, the way all peasant boys lived life in the world of Aristen, a world trapped on the verge of breaking through its medieval setting. School, chores, eating, sleeping, and being pushed around by his older siblings were the major aspects in his life. Being the youngest, he was automatically forced to do everything he was told, no matter how boring it seemed to him. Krypton was growing tired of this simplistic life. He wanted adventure. He wanted fun.

Perhaps it would have been better if he really had not wanted it all, if he had not dreamed of another world outside his own, full of excitement. Everything would be as it had been. Life would be simple, yet pure. The past, however, refuses to be altered.

Chapter One

"Krypton!" Mother yelled from downstairs, "Get up now and feed the horses!"

With a groan of reluctance, Krypton sluggishly rolled off his blanket. He felt the cold pine floor through his t-shirt and shorts; but even the chill of the floor was not enough to awaken his lethargic muscles. The night had brought on a peculiar dream that he had not wanted to abandon just yet. He had been outside a castle, when his vision blurred and turned black. Instead of awaking from his dream, a golden stream of blurriness flowed over the blackness. They might have been words...

"Krypton, now!" came his mother's shout again.

"Okay, I'm up!" Krypton half yelled and half yawned down the stairs. He proceeded to stand and stretch, careful not to hit the low ceiling and window above his head. It was August 27th, the day before his sixteenth birthday.

Krypton shuffled over to the pile of clean clothes where he routinely picked out a pair of khaki shorts that were tattered, a reflection of the chores of the owner. A plain white t-shirt lay underneath, also worn thin by the hours of stable work it had experienced. Lastly, he shoved his feet into his leather work shoes. He dressed in a sort of sleeping trance. Usually, he was allowed to sleep in on the days he did not have to go to school and therefore wondered why today was different. After he was dressed, but still partially asleep, Krypton continued his shuffle down the wooden stairs and into the house's living room. Lazily, he turned the corner into the kitchen and found his three sisters and mother preparing breakfast, as expected.

All three of Krypton's sisters were older than he. They were Mother's favorites. He despised the three of them so much that one might actually call it hatred. They were so different from him. This morning Cyan was mixing the pancake batter. She had deep, blue eyes and brown hair; she was also the oldest child. Since she was twenty-two, Cyan was eligible to leave the house. Why she stayed, no one could really understand. Krypton often took to teasing her that she would not move out because she had no one to move in with. Friend or boyfriend, she did not have one.

Probably because of her stuck up personality, he mused.

Mia and Kay were identical twins. They were inseparable, never seen apart from each other. Both had brown eyes and golden hair, like Mother. Mia and Kay were always finishing each other's sentences and plotting evil schemes to "get him." The "him" was always Krypton. For a while, when he was younger, they had Krypton convinced that he was adopted. They were eighteen, and this morning they were setting the large rectangular table with silverware and plates.

"It's about time you woke up!" Cyan snapped.

Leaning against the doorway, Krypton casually stuck his hands in the pockets of his pants, still trying to wake up. "Sorry, I didn't know it was a crime to get at least seven hours of sleep," he replied. Mia and Kay rolled their eyes at the statement, but Cyan opened her mouth to argue.

"Hush, you two," Mother said as she stepped in front of the two of them with a fresh bowl of berries in her hands. "Krypton, you know better than to argue with your sisters."

Krypton scowled deeply at Cyan, knowing she would not disobey Mother and start to argue as he might have. "Yeah, I know," he muttered, just barely audible. Mia and Kay snickered at his forced surrender. The truth was, it was still too early in the morning to argue with Mum.

"Then next time think before you speak," Mother scolded. She placed the berries on the table and hurried back over to the fire-lit stove.

"Now go out to the stables and help Father, Terrence, and Colton. Be quick! They might not have finished yet."

With a shrug, Krypton abandoned his shuffle and finally walked out the old back door. The Ight's house was one of the few two-story houses in the village. The downstairs consisted of four rooms. The largest room was the living room. It held the front door, which lead out onto the front lawn and Main Street. The kitchen held the back door leading to the family's stables. The third room was the bathroom, a small doorway under the stairs, and beyond the forbidden door in the bathroom was where Krypton's parents slept. They kept their room locked at all times. Upstairs there were only two rooms with a door and wall separating them. The top step led directly to the boys' room. Krypton and his brothers, Terrence and Colton, kept their personal belongings there and shared the floor on which they slept. Across the room and through the door was the girls' room where his sisters slept. The boys were not allowed in there, so Krypton had no idea what that room was like. In the boys' room there were two windows. One was on the wall facing the alley between the Ight's house and their neighbor's and the other was a skylight on the low ceiling.

The back door swung shut with a loud bang causing Krypton to flinch. The hinges were still rusty beyond belief and Krypton had not gotten use to the new exit alarm. Now fully awake thanks to a quickened heartbeat and fresh air, he spotted his father exiting the stables.

The Ights raised horses for a living and each of them had their own horse at this time. Mother's and Father's horses were both white stallions named Peace and Trinity. Cyan's dark-coated mare was named Black Raven, even though it was not really black, as she preferred to pretend. Colton and Terrence had a sleek black mare and a rough gray stallion whose names were Siena and Tuck, respectively. Mia and Kay owned two pinto mares. Mia's was named Café (It looked like coffee and sugar.) and Kay's was named Seqdina. She claimed it meant *Mixture* in her own weird language. Selling the horses' offspring to other villagers was their trade and their only means of income.

Of course, Krypton held the opinion that his horse was the best of them all. He may have been just a two-year old, but the colt was large and strong. Father gave Krypton responsibility over the deep-colored bay for his fourteenth birthday, the same day the colt had been born. Father named him Starchaser, Star for short because he was born in the middle of the clearest night he had ever seen. Krypton loved him and always spent as many hours as he could spare with the colt. For Krypton, Starchaser was his greatest friend and the little adventure he had in his life.

"Well, there you are at long last," Father greeted Krypton. "Better hope you're not too late. Terrence and Colton are already finishing up their mucking job. You best do your chores before you owe them for doing yours." He walked by Krypton and then into the house. The back door acknowledged his entry with a bang of displeasure once again.

Father was tall, and had brown, graying hair with sky blue eyes. His moustache was graying too. He was normally good tempered, but when he became angry, everyone stayed silent. Even Terrence and Colton were afraid when Father was angry.

Terrence and Colton were twins too; they were both twenty years of age. Although they acted alike, they were not close to looking alike. Terrence was broad shouldered and muscular, with dark eyes and blonde hair. Colton had brown hair with the same sky blue eyes as Father. He was lanky and did not have much muscle, but he was still more muscular than Krypton. Both of them claimed their fame by being tricksters and as sly as foxes.

Krypton opened the barn door to spread some light in and found them both by Tuck's stall. Once Colton and Terrence spotted him, Krypton received a rather rude greeting.

"Where have you been, squirt? Sleeping in to let us do all the work?" Colton asked with a hint of anger in his deep voice as he leaned on his pitchfork.

"Well yeah, Colt, did not you know all babies of the house have to have their sleep?"

Terrence mocked Krypton, sending the ornery twins into a laughing fit.

Krypton pushed them both aside so he could get to Star's stall. "Shut up, *Terry*!" he replied angrily, knowing it would end his brother's mockery at once.

Even though his back was turned, Krypton could imagine Terrence's face turning red with furry. He hated to be called by that feminine name.

"I told you never to call me that!" he growled. When Krypton kept walking, Terrence advanced swiftly and tackled him from behind, wrestling Krypton to the ground.

"Let me go!" Krypton shouted. Terrence had pinned his arms to his side, so Krypton could only hope to kick him off balance as he swung his makeshift work boots. He could hear Colton laughing at the sight of their fight.

Terrence finally wrestled Krypton off the ground and threw him into the only empty stall in the stables. Before Krypton had the chance to even stand, Terrence had shut the sliding door and locked it.

Why do I bother staying in this household? Krypton thought to himself. A warm trickle down his chin told Krypton that Terrence had busted his lip.

"Looks like you're going to be late for breakfast," Colton chimed in as the two of them started to walk away.

"Yeah," Terrence answered, shaking the

hay off of his clothes. "Don't worry, we won't save you anything." They continued on out of the stables with broad smiles.

"Terry… ha, that was funny!" Colton muttered.

"Shut up!" Terrence growled quietly. Krypton heard an "*Oof!*" come from Colton along with the clash of buckets after Terrence pushed him into the supply corner. Krypton struggled to get up as he held back laughter.

After the two had shut the barn door, Krypton let out a sigh and pushed a hand through his hair. He was definitely the odd end of the family. With white blonde hair and ice blue eyes, he looked nothing like the rest of them. He was tall; the tallest in his class, but being the youngest of his household, all of his siblings were taller. A habit of his was to use flower sap to make his short hair spike, but this morning he had left it a matted mess on his head.

With the stable door shut, Krypton noticed it was rather dark in the barn, especially for ten in the morning with a small kerosene lamp burning. Then he realized that Colton and Terrence had left the horses' windows shut. Krypton sighed deeply again and looked for a stiff piece of straw. Once he had found one, he used a technique that he had developed from being locked in the stables once before. He casually stuck the piece of straw in the lock and twisted it until the pad clicked. The lock sprung open and allowed Krypton to quickly slide the door ajar.

Instead of going back to the house right away and surprising his brothers on how quickly he managed to escape, Krypton opened seven of the horses' stall windows before stopping at Starchaser's quarters. He ran a hand across the smooth silver horseshoe his father had nailed to the door for him. On cue, a soft snort came from inside the shadows. Starchaser greeted him with another soft snort and, as soon as Krypton had entered his stall, searched his hands and pockets for treats. Star's large, soft brown eyes looked disappointed when he found nothing.

"Hey boy," Krypton whispered as he stroked his soft nose. "I couldn't get anything for you this time. My mother and sisters were in the kitchen." Starchaser seemed to understand, so Krypton opened the window for him.

Suddenly, a loud clash sounded from the kitchen. Thinking of the kitchen brought back the memory of how delicious the pancakes had smelled when he came down the stairs this morning. Remembering the smell also reminded Krypton of how hungry he was. With a quick goodbye to Star, Krypton shut the stall door. The colt stuck his head out the window as Krypton ran down the isle, startling the other horses. He shut the stable door and saw Starchaser poke his head out the window. The house was only a few meters from the stables, so it did not take long to get to the back door.

Chapter Two

Yet again, the old screen door slammed shut as Krypton entered the kitchen. Colton was picking up a broken ceramic plate from the floor while Terrence sat with an amused smile on his face.

"You're late Krypton," said Terrence as Krypton stepped over the fragments.

"Yes, Krypton, what kept you?" Cyan asked in her demanding tone. Mia and Kay sat at the table giggling silently as Father watched Colton to make sure he disposed of all the glass. Colton's eyes widened in fear that Krypton would tell on them, but who would believe him if he did?

"I was opening the horses' windows and Café's window was stuck," Krypton lied. "Anyway, what happened here?"

Mother walked into the kitchen and answered, "Colton thought he would get the first bits of food, but burned himself on the fire and dropped his plate." She sighed.

"Oh," was all Krypton managed to reply, holding back laughter while he sat down at the table. *Colton is having a rough day.*

"Do not forget to shut those windows tonight, Krypton," Father continued. "It is supposed to storm, not a bad storm, but all the same, I don't want the horses to have wet bedding."

Mother finished pouring everyone a drink and placed the food on the table. "Sorry it's late, but then again, better late than never."

Personally, Krypton was glad it was late; otherwise he would not have been sitting there eating it, silent as an obedient dog. During meals they were not supposed to talk unless directed. Krypton sat and ate his pancakes with a bit of excitement. He was waiting for someone to bring up tomorrow, his birthday. Each time someone coughed, he jumped a little, but was disappointed each time. This breakfast was slow and silent. Once it was over, Krypton grabbed everyone's empty plates and took them over to the sink. It was his turn to wash.

As the syrup and remains of the pancakes reluctantly relinquished their hold on the ceramic plates, Krypton had a continuous thought throbbing in his mind. *This life is too boring; everyday is the same, no adventure. Everything is just dull.* He glanced into the living room where his family was relaxing, as per usual. By the time he finished, Krypton's siblings would be going to work or school like they did every day. Luckily, Krypton did not have to be bored by school today.

It was at that moment Krypton knew what he wanted for his birthday. He wanted adventure, excitement, and to be out of this dull household with all of the same routines every single day. He finished the dishes quietly with that happy, wishful thought, and then entered the living room to join his family.

"Could I take Star out for exercise, Mother?" he asked after a few minutes of tortured silence. Already he needed to get out of the house and breathe.

"Of course, but be back before dinner," she said from behind her book.

Krypton decided to avoid slamming the back door and went out the front instead. The few flowers Mother had planted out front in the flowerbeds were starting to wilt. It seemed cold for August, as if autumn had come early. Krypton enjoyed the solace of walking alone down the alley toward the backyard, until Terrence and Colton came up behind him.

"Mother says we have to follow you into town, but don't worry, we're going to work, not just to hang around with you," Terrence sneered.

"Yeah, we won't grace you with our presence for too long," Colton added, which caused the two of them to start laughing, again. Krypton scowled at their ill-formed humor and hurried to Star's stall.

Starchaser seemed very excited to see

him when Krypton arrived at the horse's stall. He began to playfully paw the dirt ground, so Krypton calmed him with a few sugar cubes he had stolen from the kitchen while doing the dishes. Soon, Starchaser was content and saddled with Krypton mounted on his back.

Outside the barn, Colton and Terrence were already waiting for them on Siena and Tuck. The trio trotted through the alley again, Star and Krypton bringing up the rear, and onto the large dirt road of Main Street.

Krypton kept Star in the center of the road so he would not go after the produce the merchants were selling. There were severe penalties for stealing goods, and if the thief were a homeless kid or any citizen living off the streets, law enforcers would likely kill him or her. Villagers did not stand for crime. They feared it would spread faster than fire if left unpunished. However, as much as crime was feared, the fear of fire was far greater. The houses behind the produce stands were extremely close together, some roofs even touched. There was great risk of a massive, potentially deadly, fire.

Tuck and Siena slowed and turned into the blacksmith's shop where Colton and Terrence worked. Being younger, Krypton had to wait until they dismissed him before he could leave their presence. The twins tied their horses to a pole and walked under the tent.

"Hey, Mick!" Terrence yelled. "We're here!"

From the shadows in the back, an old grizzly man with black smudges on his face and a shiny, bald head came limping. "It's about time!" he said in a wheezy voice. "Get to work now. I got a large demand for shoeing today. Some man up the road needs new shoes for all ten of his horses."

"You can leave now, squirt," Colton told Krypton as he put on thick leather gloves and his scorched apron.

Krypton frowned at the name-calling, but sat up in the saddle at the pleasant thought of leaving the two jerks. He pushed Star on toward the edge of town and the Divides Forest that separated the land of Aristen into east and west. Inside the Divides and just north of Main Street lay Krypton's secret hangout, an old abandoned apple orchard.

Chapter Three

The sky was beginning to grow darker with
each passing minute; Father's prediction about a
storm had been correct. The dirt forest trail was
enveloped in the shadows of the surrounding
oak trees. The silence was almost spooky. The
only sounds that stirred were the tinkering of the
dead leaves littering the ground before Krypton
and Star, swirling around in the afternoon breeze.
Starchaser trotted rather reluctantly.

Once the path opened and ended, Star
stepped onto a small, lush green field with a
single apple tree. The scene looked almost
enchanting. He had discovered the area when
he had been younger and snuck away from his
parents' sight. The little meadow had obviously
been forgotten in the dark Divides Forest. The
trees had been ill cared for and the apples were
never picked. Finally, all but one tree had died.
Krypton took to keeping the last tree alive and

had been rewarded with luscious red apples every year since.

Krypton dismounted and unsaddled Star so he could lie down on the soft grass. The colt did too, almost immediately, under the tree. The shade of the apple tree seemed warmer than the shade of the storm clouds. Out of habit, Krypton took hold of one of the lower braches of the apple tree and swung himself into the leaves and blossoms. He picked two bright red apples from the branches before climbing back down and giving one to Star. Krypton took a large bite out of the other. The fruit was cool and refreshing. As soon as he had situated himself on the grass under the tree, Krypton leaned back to rest on Star's back. The apple was gnawed to the core and then thrown into the woods for the squirrels. With a heavy sigh of comfort, Krypton found himself looking high up to the heavens beyond the darkening sky. Star's steady heartbeat soon had him fast asleep. Krypton's dream was even stranger than the night before.

Again, he was standing in front of a castle for the longest time, just looking up at the many spires and towers. Then, the vision changed and he found that he had been transferred to the interior of a shabby-looking house. On the floor was a mysterious glowing green circle. He tried to reach down and touch the anomaly.

Krypton bolted upright and awake. A loud but low rumble of thunder trilled across the meadow. The sky was as dark as though sunset had passed. Storm clouds fumbled over one another as a fierce wind blew them into the direction of town.

"Oh no, I slept too long! It's surely past dinner time now!" Krypton mumbled aloud as he feared his mother's wrath for being tardy. Starchaser was no longer lying under the tree. He was nudging the saddle. He also knew it was time to leave.

Quickly, Krypton re-saddled and remounted his steed. Star reared with a loud snort before pouncing upon the ground and taking off through the Divides Forest. Krypton urged him on with a wild fear of what awaited him at home. They raced through the dark, wooded trail as the wind whipped hard into their faces. Once they were finally clear of the mighty shield of oak trees, the whipping wind intensified. Down empty Main Street they raced without any hint of tiring, slowing just in time to turn the corner into the alley by the Ights' house. Krypton slid off Starchaser's back, saddle and all, and threw open the barn door, seemingly before they had even stopped. Star hurriedly trotted back into his stall. The windows were already closed. He seemed grateful to lie down on fresh hay, knowing he was safe from the impending storm. Another roar of thunder boomed distantly overhead.

Reluctant to go inside, Krypton's mind began formulating ideas and excuses for being late. Finally, he settled on trying to creep quietly through the back door and sneak upstairs unnoticed. He walked gently up to the back door and opened it without so much as a squeak. His heart, thumping loudly in his throat, distracted him. He let go of the door once he set foot in the kitchen. The screen and metal slammed into the framed. Within a second, seven pairs of eyes were staring at him from the living room.

"Um… sorry, I'm late?" he suggested.

"Krypton Ight!" Mother shouted as she got up from her chair. "Do you know what time it is?"

"…past dinner time?" Krypton replied. Her expression turned to fury. Krypton looked at his work boots in shame. "I'm sorry, I fell asleep…."

"Hold your tongue! How could you fall asleep? Where in the world did you go?"

Her voice became louder, but Krypton stayed silent, not wanting to give away the location of his hideaway. No doubt his siblings would want to claim it for themselves and their friends. Through his silence he heard Colton and Terrence snickering softly, though the girls were looking rather serious about the matter.

"Fine, if you do not want to talk, march straight up to your room! You can eat in the morning!"

At moments like these, he knew better than to protest, so reluctantly walked up the stairs to the dark second floor. Krypton stood under the glass window for a moment, his rage boiling like the thunderclouds in front of him.

Furiously, he kicked a pillow across the room, but then felt his own humiliation as he realized he needed to retrieve it before lying down in his blanket space. Krypton stared hard at the skylight above him, watching the dark clouds roll with his own anger. He fell asleep with that anger in his head and in his heart. Krypton may have been angry with himself for letting the time slip by, but he also felt angry with his family, and their monotonous way of life. Krypton found himself wishing for a better life more than ever now.

The dream returned for the duration of his sleep. It was blurred; he still could not make out the golden words running through his mind.

Chapter Four

Krypton awoke to the hourly tolls from the bell at the small church on Main Street. It was ten p.m. Nothing specifically had woken him, not even the thunder that boomed overhead now with full force. He had just found himself awake. His brothers were snoring loudly, so he knew he would not get back to sleep in the small room. Krypton quietly stood and walked over to the window on the wall. He opened it, careful not to awaken his brothers. Krypton tied his blanket to the support beam in the middle of the room, not too tight, just firm enough to hold his weight. Once it was secure, and he was satisfied, Krypton flung the linen out the window and descended expertly. It was not the first time he had escaped in this manner.

Once Krypton reached the bottom, the extremely loud thunder caused him to flinch. Although sounding loud in his upstairs room,

Krypton realized the rumbles had been muffled by the indoor insulation... and my brothers' snores; he chuckled at the thought. The storm seemed to be directly above the town now, but the rain had not yet arrived. Krypton pulled the blanket free of the knot and slung it over his shoulder again. After a quiet shuffle to the stables, he slowly slid the door open and crept inside. The sweet smell of hay invaded his nostrils as he passed the other stalls down the narrow path to Starchaser.

Star greeted him with a soft whinny, but laid his head back down and closed his eyes immediately after. As he had done so many times before, Krypton spread his blanket out and leaned on Star's back, just as he had done in the meadow. He gently fell back asleep even with the storm roaring overhead.

Chapter Five

Crash! The booming thunder woke Krypton some time later. His first concern was to remember where he was, but Starchaser violently smashing his hooves against the stall door was enough to remind him. Krypton rubbed the sleep from his eyes, blinked a few times, and noticed an eerie, red glow pulsating through the cracks in the wood that formed the stable. It was the same sinister glow he had seen from the stove after burning himself the other day… Fire! Lightning must have struck a house down the road, setting it ablaze. The fire would surely spread through the nearby houses that were nestled so closely together.

Krypton leapt up from his blanket and slipped on the straw before spilling out of Starchaser's stall. He quickly opened all the other horses' stalls. If his house were on fire, then the barn might be in danger of going up in flames, as well. Krypton quickly shook the vision of his burning home from his mind. No matter how mundane his life seemed, it was still home. He could not stop to think about the horrible possibilities. Krypton knew he had to act swiftly and responsibly if he were to save anyone or anything.

The horses charged from the barn as soon as Krypton had the largest sliding door opened. To escape the commotion, they ran in every direction which startled Krypton. He dodged a white blur -it might have been Peace or Trinity- and then tripped and fell onto dry ground; the rain still had not begun to fall. When the thundering of hooves passed and the crashing thunder took its place, Krypton bravely looked up from the ground. He found it necessary to shield his adjusting eyes from the bright red and orange light flickering menacingly before him. Krypton's house was on fire!

"No…" he mouthed as a wave of horror washed over him before he scrambled to his feet.

Everything was engulfed in flames. Krypton hurriedly tried to open the back door. He tugged and pulled, but the door did not budge.

For all the times it could have been stuck, why does it have to be now? He knew from experience, it was futile to stay and try to open it. Krypton cursed and kicked the door ferociously. Furry accompanied the fear that now fueled his action. He grabbed the nearest rock, one about the size of his fist, and slung it toward the kitchen window next to the defective door. The glass shattered and rained down to the floor on the other side in a cascade of reddish glimmers. Krypton took a large breath of fresh air and then leaped through the flames and broken glass into the deadly red light.

The smoke was thick and accumulating fast around Krypton. He coughed and sputtered as he kneeled on the kitchen floor, trying to search for a sign of life, a sign of movement. No one was in the kitchen. Krypton tried to stand, but found the smoke to be too thick. He bent himself over, coughing up a storm to match the one still booming in the sky. He made his way out of the kitchen. Everywhere he looked was lit red and hazy. For a moment Krypton grew wary of becoming lost in his own home. He stumbled into the living room where just earlier his entire family had scolded him with unsettling gazes. The first sight he saw was the stairs to his and his sibling's sleeping rooms. The wooden steps were totally ablaze. No one would have survived getting down from there. Through another stream of coughing, Krypton prayed that his family was already outside.

Creeeeeeeeeeeack! A falling rafter missed Krypton's head by inches. He dove away as a flame licked his arm. It hurt far worse than when he had burned himself on the stove. Another *creeeeeeack* threatened and Krypton realized then that he could not stay and search for his family much longer. He located the front door through the haze and forced it open.

The air was considerably clearer once he tripped down the front steps onto the patchy front lawn. He lay facedown in a fit of coughing and found himself listening to the town around him crackle with fire and boom with thunder. The town's people were running and screaming, crying over lost lives and property.

Krypton found himself standing with shaking knees. He was the only Ight standing on the front lawn, with mouth slightly agape and eyes widened in shock. His home, his life, and his family burned to the ground and collapsed in a few crackles, becoming nothing but hot ashes and loose timber. It was as if the same pull of gravity that pulled the house also pulled the patient rain from the swollen and darkened clouds above the town. The cold splashes did little to calm the raging fires. The church, not left out from the merciless heat, began to chime its bells again. It was fifteen minutes past twelve o'clock. A lonely thought flashed through Krypton's mind.

Happy birthday to me…

Chapter Six

Krypton spent only a few moments standing in the bone chilling rain before feeling a soft nuzzle upon his shoulder. He turned around to see Starchaser with his head hung low, a saddened expression along with fright in his large brown eyes. Krypton patted him softly, burying his face in Star's silky, but soaking wet mane. The two shared a sense of silent despair, mourning over what had just transpired. The heat of his crumbled house was becoming unbearable, along with the pain of the cold, pounding rain and sadness. Krypton mounted Star bareback and let him take them both out of town by way of the back streets. They dared not go to the apple tree or its memories. Little hope for Krypton's family surviving was left; they were nowhere to be seen, and would not be seen again.

No one lived on the backstreets that led through the Divides and into the other towns of Aristen, so the noise of screaming and crying soon diminished to a silent hum. Krypton could not distinguish the pouring rain from the tears rolling down his cheeks. Even Star trucked along with his head lowered in despair. The feeling that time had stopped fell upon them as they walked the muddy path.

When Krypton could no longer cry, he found questions of forlornness formulating in his mind. Although he tried, it seemed impossible to answer them. *Where will we go? What will we do now? What should we do?*

At least they had escaped the village. Children on their own were put in group homes until they were shoved out the door once they became of age.

I would be better off dead than in one of those homes for boys, thought Krypton. *The town's people will believe me dead anyway since my whole home and family had been destroyed. Nobody would guess that I had survived by sleeping in the barn.*

For a few hours, Krypton thought of his past life, letting the memories overflow the questions. He began to remember the fun times there had actually been. Finally, his thoughts came to rest on his childhood and an antic he played when he was younger. Krypton recalled pretending to be a master-mind criminal as a hobby. He stole food from his brothers' plates, but replaced it later after they were confused by the sudden disappearance. It always worked and was very amusing for Krypton.

Another thought occurred to Krypton. What if he could become the ultimate outlaw? *I could go anywhere I wanted at any time. I could visit other towns, other countries, or even other worlds.*

In grade school, Krypton had been taught that there were no worlds other than Aristen, the world in which he lived. But he had been suspicious from the beginning about the strict regulation against speaking of other worlds. Though recently, rouge scientists had been developing ways to transport, negating the belief of Aristen as the only world. The people of Aristen had to admit the fact that they were not the sole inhabitants of the universe. Rapidly, Aristen began to industrialize through the influence of other worlds. Krypton remembered when his young and bold geography teacher suddenly turned to discuss what other worlds besides Aristen might be like. Krypton's attention was astute as the possibility of modern transportation to other worlds was hinted. There had to be an up-to-date method to get to these other worlds somewhere; scientists were making breakthroughs every day.

Feeling a little optimistic with this hopeful thought in his mind, Krypton steered Star to the side of the road nearest the forest as the clouds began to lift and the rain move on.

A glorious morning overtook the sky in the next few hours. The sun glared through the clouds and treetops as though trying to make up for the rainstorm overnight. Krypton had

to hold up a hand to shade his eyes. He clicked
to Starchaser with his tongue and his faithful
friend walked to their left and into the forest.
They found a small clearing deep within the
shadows where an old tree had been uprooted.
Krypton decided then that if he was going to
be an outlaw, he should start by traveling at
night. Krypton dismounted and gave Star the
majority of the clearing to lie down and rest; he
sat down next to the rotting bark of the oak. Star
followed suit, laid down, and snoozed in the soft
dirt. Krypton assumed they could both become
accustomed to a nocturnal lifestyle. Though
the shade of the trees was cool, the sun began to
calmly heat the forest. Krypton was soon asleep
in its comfort.

Nightmares flooded his dreams. Krypton
saw the fire again and his home crashing to
the ground. He could hear the screams from
the town. He could hear the crackle of timber.
Krypton felt like he was spinning out of
control, he could not take it any more! He was
completely helpless. Through all of the misery,
he heard his mother scream. Krypton's mind fell
into an endless black void until finally he awoke
with a jolt, sweat dripping down his face. It was
dark again, but just barely. Star was munching
a bit of grass and snorted when he saw that
Krypton was awake.

Still disturbed by his dreaming, Krypton
could not speak a word, but climbed up onto
Stars back telling him it was time to continue

moving. The sky was clear and full of stars, not a cloud in the sky. Krypton and Starchaser continued on down the road they had begun the day before. It was cold again. Krypton's skin developed goose bumps even under the t-shirt, and cargo pants he had donned the morning before. He had not bothered to change into sleepwear that night. Star also shivered slightly. After a few hours of nighttime traveling, they approached a wooden sign on the opposite side of the road. It was dark out, but Krypton could still read it.

AnDev, the capital of Aristen
(Home of Lonely Castle and Scientists around the world)
10 km straight ahead, through Myron Town

Under it was another sign that had been newly placed there:

Sir Casente will be performing a demonstration of his new Teleportor on August 29th.

"August 29th?" Krypton asked himself aloud. "That's tomorrow, unless it happens to be past midnight already, then it's today. Maybe, if this teleportor isn't a fake, I can use it to get to other worlds."

This was his chance to find those other worlds that only heretics spoke of. Perhaps in AnDev they were more lenient towards scientists.

They must be if the Casente scientist has been knighted, Krypton thought.

Star broke into a gallop so they could reach Myron Town faster and before sunrise. Krypton had heard from others at school that the system of punishment there was also strict. In this case, school had been good for something. Stationed inside the town was the highest ranking jail of Aristen. Here they did not bother sorting out small crimes from serious ones. The jailers just wanted to fill the cells and empty them again quickly. Criminals who committed serious or deadly crimes from all over were placed in the cells until put to death. So, if a person were caught committing a crime in the town, no matter how low ranking it was, he or she might be sentenced to death.

Just as the sun began to peek over the horizon, Star stepped through the gates to Myron Town. It was a small town despite the size of the jail looming in the distance. A wide dirt street laid through the town, announcing itself the main road, and stretched all the way to the next town, the capital of Aristen, AnDev. Starchaser and Krypton found that they blended in perfectly with the large crowd. The only problem was, as they drew closer to the end of the large road, and passed the two story jail, the duo began to spot more and more food stands. Fruits and vegetables lined the carts, as well as the occasional meat cart.

A tight knot formed in Krypton's stomach as he and Star continued down the crowded road, passing consumers on foot and on horseback like himself. The scent of produce tauntingly wafted through the air and Star shivered below Krypton, this time not with cold, but with a sweet tooth. He was as hungry as Krypton was, even though he had nibbled grass in the forest. Krypton started to search his pockets for any money he could have possibly left in them, but stopped almost immediately. He decided it was time to begin practicing a new life. He would take what he and Star needed; he did not have any money anyway.

Pretending as though he were tired of riding bareback, Krypton dismounted Star and led him to the side of the road. He pressed a slightly shaking finger to his lips and told Star to stay and wait there for him. Then, ever so cautiously, Krypton slipped to the far side of a fruit stand.

Bright red apples lay in a brown crate, just inches from his hands. Their red glow was almost the same as the fruit of his hideout, as though it were fate that he try and take these apples and regain the memories of some of the good in his life. They seemed to bulge out of their crate towards him teasingly. A bead of sweat dribbled its way down his forehead, but he overcame his own anxiety and bumped purposely into the cart. Krypton ducked out of view as the caretaker of the cart glanced his way briefly, before stumbling to grab a box of oranges that were threatening to fall off the stand. Quick as a cat, and as though by instinct, Krypton grabbed two of the gleaming apples from the crate and concealed them in his hands.

The commotion ceased shortly after Krypton had taken a few steps away from the cart; the oranges had been saved. All Krypton needed to do was get back to Starchaser without looking conspicuous. The only thing between the two of them was a cart of assorted brass accessories and an old woman watching over it. Behind her was a small child. A wave of triumph, a realization of success, swept over Krypton, who began to walk a little quicker. Star picked up his ears upon seeing the smile on Krypton's face. He was almost there…

Just as Krypton stepped into the path of the accessory cart, the child behind the old woman rolled a brass plate out into the street in front of Krypton. He did not see it until it was so close that it was too late to stop. Krypton toppled over the plate, half tripping over his own feet in an awkward attempt to halt himself. Unable to limit his fall with his hands, Krypton's body hit the dirt road heavily.

The apples flew from his hands at the same moment Krypton heard someone yell about apples missing from a cart. More yelling erupted as his face hit the ground. He had been discovered! Remembering the system of justice, Krypton decided that he really needed to get off the ground and get out of there, now. He threw dust up from the road underneath him and scrambled over to Star who was racing his way, sensing danger. Krypton left the apples behind, leapt up onto Star's back, parted the crowd in the street, and twisted around buildings on the lesser-traversed roads.

Besides the steady racing hoof beats of Star and his own heart beat, Krypton heard the clanking of armor behind them accompanied by even more hoof beats. Justice Knights were gaining on the two of them, and quickly. Krypton risked a glace over his shoulder and noticed that these knights had strange metal barrels in their hands.

"I told you this town was crazy, Star! It looks like we won't be eating here," Krypton joked half-heartedly as the knights began to drift back on the long road. Starchaser was much faster than their horses.

A loud bang suddenly rang in his ears and a sharp wind skimmed Krypton's head. Something had just barely missed him. Krypton looked over his shoulder once more. The metal barrels were being aimed at them from behind.

"What in the heck was that?" he asked himself.

In the same second Krypton spoke, he heard another shot and a piercing sensation flooded his left arm, slowly making its way through his body. Star stumble after another shot was fired. Everything blurred, but Krypton identified the ground racing up to meet him. He felt the horrible impact as both he and Starchaser crashed to the dusty earth.

When the dazed feeling left his brain and was replaced with pain, Krypton opened his eyes. A pool of dark blood was forming from a wound in his arm. Star was motionless on his left. Krypton slowly crawled over to him, fearing the worst, but not wanting to believe it. Starchaser's right, front leg was in an awkward position; it had broken in the fall. There was also a wound on his torso that was similar to the one on Krypton's arm. Krypton held Star's soft face in his good arm and wept silently for his best friend.

The knights had finally caught up to Krypton and his felled steed. One each grabbed him by an arm; the wounded one drenched by another wave of blood and pain. Krypton cringed as he was led away from the only member of his family who had survived the fire. He did not want to believe it, but Star was gone, and it was his fault. Misery landed in his heart; a misery so heavy that he did not bother to struggle against the knight's pull. Krypton realized he was going to miss the teleportor demonstration, but right now, it really did not seem to matter. Nothing but Star's death mattered anymore. Krypton's plan to escape Aristen had ended, and with the greatest pessimism he had felt since the fire, he told himself that life would only get worse before better, if it would get better at all.

Chapter Seven

Krypton was taken to the large jail where he would wait until a trial was scheduled, just like all the other criminals. After being thrown into the cold dungeon cell, he sat quietly in the corner and cradled his bloodied arm with care, watching the rats creep across the floor, listening to the moans of other prisoners. It baffled him that they could do this to *any* kid. Every so often, for about the next three hours, a prisoner would be dragged away to his death, praying out loud or screaming for mercy. It sent shivers up and down Krypton's spine. This was not his idea of a happy birthday.

The guard that had been sitting on a stool by the wooden door next to a rack of keys, finally stood and left as another man came to take his place for the night. Another screaming prisoner was carried out with him. Krypton shivered once more before leaning back on the wall, attempting to rest.

Dreams came flooding into his mind like never before. Krypton could recognize a window, a barred window. Outside of it, birds were chirping. Krypton's vision turned yellow, but he saw the huge castle before him when the confusion cleared. He came closer to it... and closer... and closer yet... before a swirling mass of black and white swallowed Krypton's vision and sent him back into the cold depths of a black abyss! Krypton heard himself scream. He felt himself fall.

Creeeeeack! The wooden door to the cells slammed shut around six in the morning, judging by the sunrise through the barred windows. The sudden noise caused Krypton to jump from his sleep, scraping his arm on the wall, sending a fresh wave of pain through his bicep and spilling more blood to the floor. Krypton felt his face; it was cold, clammy, and dripping sweat. Another guard had just entered; although he did not look well. Perhaps he was just not yet awake.

This guard's clothes were badly tattered. He was a total slob. His eyes drooped and he did not seem to be able to walk straight. Krypton stood up and leaned on the barred door to get a better look at him. The guard was attempting to sit on the stool, but fell off the side and chuckled lightly. Krypton frowned in disgust as the guard tried again and finally succeeded. It was then that Krypton found the answer to the guard's strange behavior. After the guard had sat down, he scanned the area, reached slowly into his jacket pocket and removed a glass bottle. The potent smell that packed the air around the jail told Krypton immediately that the guard had just uncorked a bottle of alcohol. He took a long swig and then carefully returned the bottle to his pocket and hiccupped.

Hey, wait, Krypton began to think to himself, *if this guy is drunk, maybe I can get a few things out of him.*

"Excuse me, sir," Krypton said to the guard.

The guard looked around, confusion apparent on his face, before he saw Krypton and smiled. "Why *-hic-* hello, boy," he replied in a drunken voice.

"Hello," Krypton replied. "I was wondering if you know anything about the teleportor demonstration that took place yesterday. I seemed to have missed it."

The guard gurgled a bit before saying, "You're sentenced to *-hic-* death you know."

Krypton rolled his eyes at the guard's stupidity, but decided to go with it. "Oh! That's terrible! I can't believe they can do that to kids like me. I'm just a homeless boy looking for food, after all. They did something to my arm and killed my horse with strange little metal barrels."

"Aw, now *-hic-* that's a sad story there. Them metal barrels are called guns. *-hic-* They shoot lead *-hic-* bullets. I specialize in fixing them *-hic-* wounds. You say you got *-hic-* hit?" he replied.

"Why, yes. Here, on my arm." Krypton held his wounded arm through the bars on his cell door. The guard left his stool and wobbled toward Krypton.

He opened the cell door with the keys he picked up from the hook in the wall, but Krypton did not run. As of now, he did not have anywhere to go and he could still try to get information from this drunkard.

"Ah, this –*hic*- isn't very bad," the guard told him with his face in Krypton's after examining the wound. His breath was foul, and his beard unclean. Krypton did not mean to be a neat freak, but this guy was just plain dirty. Krypton held his breath for as long as he could.

He began to squeeze the bleeding wound, making Krypton want to shout out in pain. He held his tongue, however. A pressure in the wound lifted just as a small clink sounded from the floor. Looking down, Krypton saw the bullet the guard had talked about, a small black circle. Krypton was baffled at how a small piece of lead such as that had killed Starchaser. Using a bit of cloth from Krypton's ripped shirt, the guard continued to dress the wound. Soon, the scrap of fabric was stained with a patch of blood, but it felt better. The guard turned and exited the cell, locking it behind him. He carelessly sat back down on the stool with keys in hand.

"Masterful," Krypton complimented somewhat sarcastically, not meaning to put too much pride into the drunken man.

"I thank –*hic*- you. Not like it'll –*hic*- matter. You'll be dead 'fore luncheon," he chuckled, taking another drink.

"Yes, it's a pity," Krypton mumbled, a bit irritated at being reminded of his death. He decided to take another stab at the first question he had asked. "Do you know anything about Sir Casente and his teleportor demonstration?"

"Aye, that I –*hic*- do!" the guard replied. Krypton perked up knowing that he was getting somewhere now. The guard continued, "I went to the –*hic*- dermonstra-thingy. Load of phooey though. Casente –*hic*- said you have to be immortal to use the silly green circle. I told him –*hic*- that it was pish-posh and he gave me this here gin." He held the bottle up so Krypton could see and then continued.

"And he told me that if I didn't get drunk drinking it, and did not have a hangover –*hic*-, then I was right about the teleportor. But if I did get sick after drinking it, he was right. Well, before that I had told him that I never get drunk, and that –*hic*- is the truth! I even dared to drink it on the job! Who do you –*hic*- thinks going to win this?" he chuckled again after taking another long swig.

"Oh, you for sure," Krypton replied again sarcastically. Sir Casente obviously knew how to deal with people who were unintelligent. Perhaps that meant he was intelligent himself. "So where is the teleportor? And how can someone become immortal? It seems like a rather odd task to want to accomplish."

"If you're looking for the *–hic–* teleportor you're in luck. That character Sir Casente lives in the next town over *–hic–* westward." He pointed in some strange direction, like up and right. Luckily, Krypton knew which way was west. The guard's slurred and hiccup-accompanied speech quickened, "His house lies *–hic–* where the sunset shows last. Or so he *–hic–* says." He murmured inaudibly for a second before continuing. "Becoming immortal is a tricky task boy. You could *–hic–* becomes Atherial, but that takes almost a life time to *–hic–* learn. It's like a ghost type person.

"What I suggest is going out to that *–hic–* Lonely Castle in AnDev. It's also in the same town that *–hic–* crazy Casente guy lives in." Again he pointed out into space. "To become immortal people say to enter the room behind the Door with No Handle in the west wing. Load of tarnish, though. Just like me getting drunk."

"That's interesting," Krypton muttered. He had already decided to go for the Lonely Castle idea and could also talk to Sir Casente before entering. "Okay, I have one more question."

"Ask *–hic–* away!"

"Could I borrow those keys?" Krypton asked politely as if nothing were wrong with it. A knot in his heart formed as he waited for the guard's reply. Would he really turn out to be this stupid?

The drunken guard blinked a few times… and then… well, then Krypton had to hold back laughter. The guard nodded and smiled as if he had not a care in the world about setting a prisoner free. He stood up and handed Krypton the keys! The plan could not have gone smoother.

Krypton quickly unlocked the cell door and quietly slid it open. "Thanks!" he half laughed to the man.

"Anytime. Say, there's a broken barred window –*hic*- just down the hall there." After those few, helpful words, he slid off the stool once more and fell asleep.

Krypton saluted him with another hint of sarcasm and then ran for the window with a smile on his face. On the way, Krypton noticed more prisoners who appeared to be dead, but did not stop until a wall abruptly appeared. The barred window was instantly recognizable; it was from his dream! It was just low enough that Krypton could lift himself up. The guard was right. The bars were weak and nearly broken.

After a quick look around, Krypton stood back and kicked as high and hard as he could. As he had hoped, his boot broke off the bars and let a fresh waft of dusty air flow through the musty cells.

Of course, every smoothly laid plan has a defect. When Krypton had kicked the bars, it caused them to fall to the floor with an extremely loud clatter. Immediately, he heard footsteps, footsteps of men in armor coming toward the cells, footsteps growing louder. Abruptly the wooden door flung open. Two unarmed guards stood in the doorway staring directly at Krypton.

"Stop, prisoner!" one of them yelled.

Yeah, like I'm really going to listen to that command, Krypton thought as he quickly jumped and threw himself through the window, but only managing to get half of his torso through the small opening. He struggled to find a grip on the stone wall in order to pull the rest of himself and his shoes through as the guards came running after him. He was almost out, almost free when something grabbed his ankle and began to drag him back in! The guards were attempting to pull him from the open window. Krypton dug his fingers into the dirt outside and tried to claw his way out, praying thanks that the street ahead was at the moment deserted.

He was about to give in, when his free leg hit one of the guards, knocking the law enforcer to the floor. Krypton was lifted a little higher, which sparked an idea. Instead of just knocking down the other, Krypton reeled back and slammed the soles of his shoes into the second guard who had a hold on his ankle. The force sent the guard flying back into the dungeon, and sent Krypton out the window!

Krypton rolled on the dusty ground momentarily before leaping to his feet. He heard birds singing and the clanking armor of guards becoming louder, but the afternoon sun never felt so good… *Wait a minute…guards in armor? Man, good news sure travels fast around here!* Krypton looked over his shoulder and saw them chasing after him on horseback. He scrambled as fast as he could into a run and literally dove into the next crowded street he saw, pushing his way through the sea of people.

Just as the mob of knights and guards was about to stumble upon him in the crowd, Krypton saw a cart of hay being pulled by a pair of oxen toward the west end of town. Krypton hesitated momentarily, but closed his eyes and dove into the hay. The cart wobbled hard, but the owner did not seem to notice. Holding back a sneeze, Krypton peered through the straw and found the guards looking absolutely confused. He was free of Myron Town at last.

Chapter Eight

As he lay back in the hay, Krypton inhaled the sweet scent of his concealment. It reminded him of the stables back home. Memories flooded his mind and caused Krypton's eyes to suddenly burn with tears. The warm trickle fell down his cheeks through the entire journey to AnDev

Pushing away the pain of those memories, Krypton began thinking about the task at hand. Sir Casente lived where the sunset would shine last, so it would be the farthest western house. That was where he would find the teleportor, Krypton was sure about it. Lonely Castle was conveniently built in the middle of the town, so that would not be hard to find either. The tricky part would be finding a way into the castle, but once over that hurdle, Krypton also needed to find the west wing and then the Door with No Handle. The latter was the confusing part.

How am I to get beyond the Door with No Handle if the door actually has no handle? he mused.

The question in his mind blotted out reality for most of the journey. Krypton was trying so persistently to envision opening a door without a handle that he did not even realize that the cart was slowing until it came to a lurching halt. Krypton half leapt, half fell out of the cart and quickly brushed bits of straw from his clothing. He stayed situated by the cart as the elderly driver climbed down and tipped his straw hat to his rider. Krypton casually smiled and nodded back to him. After that, his attention was captured the surroundings as the cart man began unloading the hay for a merchant's stand.

A tall wooden sign hung from the arched walkway behind Krypton, which he realized was the main entrance to the town. It read: *Welcome to AnDev!* Krypton found himself smiling. He could not believe he had made it this far in just a couple of days. In front of Krypton was the center of the town and, behind and above the many merchant stands and houses, he saw the lookout towers of Lonely Castle.

Just by seeing the tops of the towers around the outside walls, Krypton could tell it was a most magnificent castle. Despite being slightly cracked, the gray square blocks of concrete and stone were tinted with a deep blue hue. The square lookout openings were as perfect, straight, and evenly spaced as any architect could have dreamed of accomplishing. The sight could easily take away anyone's breath and cause them to crumple in awe on the cobblestone road.

The straw cart departed in a hurry, leaving Krypton coughing in a cloud of dust. Once it had cleared, he decided to take a look at the obscure base of Lonely Castle's exterior walls before paying a visit to Sir Casente.

It was a tight squeeze into the crowded streets of AnDev. People next to him did not even give the raggedly dressed boy any notice, although he must have stuck out with all of the fine clothing the residents of AnDev were accustomed to wearing. Krypton was nudged up against a fruit stand not unlike the one in Myron town. The overseer of the cart was tending to haggling with a customer. Feeling lucky, Krypton plucked an orange from the unsuspecting fruit stand. Smooth as silk; success at last. With the orange buried in his palm, Krypton squeezed between groups of shoppers and continued out of the chaos until there was only a clear road ahead. He peeled the juicy orange and savored each delicious bite.

Just as he finished devouring the tasty fruit, Krypton came to a stop at the base of Lonely Castle. He froze, mystified, as his gaze swept the castle. The outer wall stood at least five stories tall, with a drawbridge made of oak, and a moat at least a meter wide. The water appeared green, so he could not tell how deep it was, but Krypton hypothesized that something was swimming in there.

The oak drawbridge was lowered, placing a puzzled look on Krypton's face, until he noticed that one of the support chains was broken and hanging from the wall high above. A fallen drawbridge would mean easy access to treasure. Krypton suspected the reason guards were placed at the main entrance was to guard the valuables left inside; no one had lived in the castle for more than a decade. The guards had guns, too. Just looking at the weapons caused Krypton's still bandaged arm to sting again.

Krypton peered in to see the inner plaza. Green grass was growing inside and gardens of ill kept flowers lined the doorway into the castle itself. The gargoyles on the outer wall sent shivers down his spine. He wanted to look more, but snapped himself out of his trance when he realized it probably looked suspicious for a ragged looking boy to be staring up at the castle as Krypton was. He decided it was time to pay Sir Casente a visit.

Chapter Nine

It was nearing five o'clock in the afternoon when Krypton walked slowly out of the crowded market roads. People were beginning to end their shopping as he continued heading as far westward as he could. The unusually chilly August air was at it again. Krypton rubbed his bare arms gently. Stalks of tall corn loomed around the edge of the back road that he had just set foot on. He continued down the path and was led to a small cottage.

The white paint had begun to chip off the side of the house and one of the four blue window shutters was hanging limply from only one hinge. However, the smoke coming from the chimney made the place look inviting and homey.

Krypton stepped up the creaky old stairs to the front door. Like the back door back at Krypton's house, it was a screen door, and looked creaky. He opened the door and was surprised to find it was actually well-oiled. Holding his breath, Krypton knocked on the oak door that he assumed was the entryway to Sir Casente's house.

A worrisome thought hit Krypton as he let the screen door drop back into place as he waited for his unsuspecting host. Krypton realized that he had not invented a story to explain his visit. He could not tell Sir Casente that he wanted to break into the Lonely Castle. Nor could he tell the nobleman that he wanted to become immortal. Would he even let Krypton use his teleportor to reach other worlds? He heard footsteps coming toward the door and decided he would have to wing it.

The oak door creaked open. A tall, balding man in his fifties opened the screen door to get a better look at Krypton. He did not look frail or dieing like most men his age. When he smiled at Krypton he looked like a man in his twenties.

"Sir Casente?" Krypton asked the man.

"Why, yes, what can I do for you, boy?" he replied in a hearty voice. His eyes were a gray-blue color and his nose looked like it had been broken at least once. Sir Casente's fingers had a firm-looking grip to them as he pulled glasses from his shirt pocket and placed them upon his nose.

"I'm with a newly organized daily paper, and I was put in charge of an article about Lonely Castle's heritage. I was wondering if I could interview you to find out what you know about it and then tie in your new teleportor device, as well." Krypton was pleased with the story that came off the top of his head.

Sir Casente paused a moment, then replied, "Hmm, a paper? Why they don't tell anyone anything around here anymore is beyond me. When I was young, we knew what was going on and when it was happening."

"Yes, my mother once told me about the same thing," Krypton lied. "That is exactly why we are creating this paper. My employer wants you and your teleportor to be on the very first page, along with your knowledge of Lonely Castle."

Sir Casente became enveloped in thought for a moment again, making Krypton worry he might suspect something, but Sir Casente smiled again. "I'd be honored to share my knowledge. Please, please come in. It's getting cold out and standing there you look like some ragged, street boy that needs to be in a home!"

Krypton's heart flip-flopped at the thought of being discovered as he walked into the cottage rather hesitantly. Once the door slammed behind him, Krypton noticed it was almost sweltering hot in the house. The fire was strong and large in the fireplace of the lounging room they had just stepped into. The wood burner in the kitchen was burning as well. Beside the wood burner, Krypton noticed broken pipes, both hanging from the ceiling and laying in a pile on the floor below.

"My house needs a bit of fixing up," Sir

Casente said as he sat down in an armchair next to a long coffee table. He offered Krypton the one opposite him.

Krypton sat down. "I think it's a lovely house," he replied, trying endlessly to not remember how much the comfort reminded him of his own home; he did not want to break down here.

Sir Casente nodded. "I thank you, but it's really falling apart. See the pipes in the kitchen? They used to be all up in the ceiling. Now they're just weapons against anyone who tries to break in," he chuckled.

"That would get the point across to a perpetrator," Krypton replied. "Well, shall we begin?"

"Yes, yes of course, but don't you need a note pad or paper to write down what I say?"

"Err... I have a very good memory. I'll remember anything and everything you want me to." *That was a close one,* ran through Krypton's head.

"Interesting," Sir Casente mused. "Anyway, ask me anything you wish. Shall we start with the Starlington Castle?"

"Starlington Castle?" Krypton repeated. "I thought the castle's name was Lonely?"

"Lonely Castle is the nickname that was bestowed upon it when the last king and queen of Aristen were murdered on their own thrones. The true name of the castle is Starlington. The town's people believe that the royalties' ghosts still haunt the edifice today, *lonely* for their lives and ruling powers."

Krypton's curiosity perked. "...and how do you know this?"

Sir Casente cleared his throat and straightened himself in his chair. "It was my ancestors who built the castle for the monarchy," he said looking very proud. "I know everything about the castle, all of its architectural designs, and of course all the secret entrances."

"The castle has secret entrances?"

"Yes. Let me show you." He stood up and went to the kitchen.

Sounds of rustling papers and tea cups clinking met Krypton's ears. When Sir Casente returned, he held two cups and a very old rolled up piece of paper in his hands. He handed Krypton one of the cups, full of steaming tea, and sat down.

"These are the blueprints to the castle. The only reason I have them is because my ancestors built it. I find pride in that bit of my family history." Unrolling the paper he continued, "This will show the reader all the hidden doorways and entrances. Like this one," he said, pointing to a small representation of a door by the east wall. There was a rectangular dotted line around a section of the wall, and a torch was marked as the handle to the door. "This doorway will lead you to the torture chambers under the east wing, and the lower east wing has a specific hallway that leads to the west wing. It is the quickest way from one end of the castle to the other," he concluded.

"What is in the west wing, Sir?"

"Ah, yes, the west wing. In it resides that of a concealed chamber locked away behind the Door with No Handle. Although not even I know what is in the chamber, I do know that the hallway just beyond it is called the Corridor of Balance. I can also tell you that whatever is in the chamber will make you immortal."

Now Krypton felt like he was getting somewhere. "So if a person were to enter this chamber and become immortal, he would be eligible to use your teleporting device?"

"Of course, I have set up the teleportors in various worlds, for transportation, of course. However, I might add that I do not want these good townspeople to be wandering off into other worlds, so I am the only one in *this* world to have one besides the wild ones."

"Wild teleportors?"

"Yes. Wild teleportors are scattered through the worlds, but only immortals can see them, and therefore use them."

"Would it be alright for me to see your teleportor? I was told to add description to the article."

"Oh, why not, come this way."

Before Sir Casente led him to the back of the kitchen, Krypton stopped at a shelf in the lounging room and examined a strange, red contraption that had a wire wrapped with wicker sticking out of the back end of it.

"That is a firework," Sir Casente told Krypton after spotting his curious stare. "If you light that wire on fire, the red part will fly off into the sky and then burst into color and paper."

"What's the purpose of it?"

"Pure entertainment. I've seen only one in my days and was so captivated by the display that I had to own one myself. I'm saving it for a special occasion."

A firework sounds like a distraction, Krypton thought to himself. It was just big enough to fit into his pocket, too. Krypton imagined himself setting it alight and the guards running after it instead of after him when he was ready to use that secret entrance. Sir Casente was already on his way into the kitchen, so Krypton scooped up the firework and shoved it into his pocket. It was curious how quickly he was adapting to his new visage.

Krypton caught up with Sir Casente just as he reached the back of the kitchen. Here, an old wardrobe stood a few steps from the back door. It had a strange green light emanating from the cracks. Sir Casente took a small black key from his back pocket and unlocked the door. Krypton shielded his eyes from the bright green glow that emerged until his pupils had adjusted to the intensity. Inside the wardrobe was a two-dimensional, bright lime-green circle with a box shape on one side.

"I'm hoping to begin selling them to a few higher class immortals. Perhaps it will bring me money so I can fix up my house," Sir Casente smiled, as though looking upon his pride and joy. "The box on the side is where you set the coordinates of the world you would like to jump to."

As Krypton went to touch the green glowing circle, Sir Casente shut and locked the door. "If you're not immortal when you attempt to use it, you could find yourself faced with a fate worse than death. I myself have no idea what that may be, though. All I know is that the fool seems to have his soul torn apart."

"How are you able to use the teleportor then?" Krypton asked as Sir Casente led them back to the table and chairs.

They both sat back down before Sir Casente replied, "I have mastered the art of the Atherial. If I am killed, I can be reformed as energy and take human flesh and bone again. Of course it took me a very long time to do so, I'm nearing ninety now."

"But you certainly do not look it, Sir!"

"Thank you, lad. I must admit the traditional, anti-age potions we work up in the lab do wonders for me. Anyway, is that all you wanted to ask of me now?"

Krypton thought over the newly acquired information. "Yes, I think that will make a very excellent article. Thank you, Sir Casente."

"It was my pleasure, boy! Stop by any time. I would like a copy of this article when it is finished. I will surely hang it on my wall," he said, before showing Krypton to the door.

Once outside, Krypton could still hear

him mumbling about where he would put
the article. He found himself smiling again,
before realizing it was already nearly pitch dark
outside. Krypton estimated it to be around nine
o'clock, but at least he knew what he had to do
to accomplish his goal.

Chapter Ten

Krypton began a sprint to keep warm in the dark night, feeling the firework bounce against his leg. An owl's hoot broke the silence every few minutes and small lanterns flicked shadows across the buildings and houses. Soon the castle and its guards came into view.

He hid behind a barrel by the west wall, right next to the moat. If he could set this firework off farther west, it would distract the guards and send them past Krypton, giving him a clear run to the east wall and the secret entrance where the outer wall and castle touched. Entering across the drawbridge would be too risky. There could still be guards on the inside of the walls. Using the secret entrance would put him directly in the castle anyway, so he was going with the secret entrance.

After pulling the firework from his pocket, Krypton quietly grabbed two thin stones from the bank of the moat. Seeing the water ripple gave him the chills, so he quickly dried the stones off with his shirt and began to rub them together over the wick of the firework. Soon a spark lit up his face and he struck the stones together for a final time.

The firework sputtered and sparked as the wick began to burn. After Krypton had thrown it as far west as he could, he shielded his eyes while it jetted off into the air. Brilliant colors of light were emitted from the back of the firework and sounds of loud hissing and crackling were enough to pull the guards from their posts. Krypton saw his chance and dashed over to the east wall in a dead sprint. No one could have spotted him, even if they had wanted to.

The sounds of the firework died as Krypton leapt across the moat, stumbling on a narrow patch of sand before grabbing onto the blue-gray rock. Large cracks in the castle's mortar and a cluster of thick vines allowed Krypton a firm grip to pull himself to the east wall. As soon as he steadied himself, Krypton saw the torch on the wall and grabbed it. Through the dim light and behind the vines, a small, narrow opening in the wall became apparent to Krypton. He had to duck in order to step through, but he made it. Krypton was inside the castle!

Chapter Eleven

Torches lined the walls of the torture chamber in which Krypton found himself, just as Sir Casente had said. The blood of victims from years gone could be seen stained on the wooden machines. He could only imagine the horrors that had occurred here. The air was musty and thick, adding to the creepiness of the room.

Maybe the secret door had been used for removing corpses from the chamber and disposing of them in the moat, speculated Krypton. He located the stairs and exited the room, hoping never to recall the chamber again.

He was now on the ground level of the empty castle. Not even guards were allowed in here, the dust was one clue to that. It covered the velvet drapes and large framed artwork. Strangely, the works of art were all black and white, but Krypton recalled from school that the last families to live in the castle were avid collectors of water colors. Possibly, something had changed those colors… But Krypton did not have time to ponder the thought. The guards would soon be returning to their posts and he did not want his shadow lurking in the windows.

Krypton began a tip-toed walk down the corridor that Sir Casente had spoken about, searching for the stairs. The chamber had to be just above him. The dust muffled his footsteps on the black and white tiled floor, but he did not expect anyone to hear him, unless the gargoyles had ears. They stood over each doorway and seemed to stare down at Krypton with their gray, stone cold eyes. They looked like demons, demons with angel wings. Krypton was glad when he found the stairs and was relieved of their gazes.

The stairs were spiral and as soon as he stepped onto the first one, a wave of cold wind swept through him. It felt as if something above were releasing tons of energy. Continuing up the stairs, the air became colder and dustier. Krypton found himself sneezing uncontrollably once he reached the top. There dust was even thicker up here. As soon as he had finished his sneeze attack, Krypton saw his first destination: the Door with No Handle.

It was a large bronze door encrusted with all sorts of jewels, but, true to its name, it had no handle. No knob, no hinges. Although there was a lack of light in the corridor, words of silver gleamed in the shadows across the top of the door. The words read:

Seek Not Knowledge but Adventure to Unlock Your Destiny; Yet Chance Forever Unlocking Chaos Upon the World.

A new obstacle… he thought. It seemed that if Krypton obtained access into what lied behind this door, chaos could be unlocked upon the world. However, he had come this far, and was not turning back now because of a chance. Adventure was what he had wanted, and the world somehow meant little to Krypton at the moment.

The bronze of the door looked strangely smooth. No common welder could have achieved a feat such as this. Krypton cautiously reached out a hand to touch the door, but felt a shock send itself through his body. His response was to try and pull his hand away, but it would not budge, as if magnetically attached!

"Ah! Let go!" He struggled to pull his palm off the door. Suddenly, his vision went black and the words… the words from his dreams flashed through his head. Krypton found himself saying them aloud.

Dies irea, Dies illa,
Solvet saeclam in favilla,
Teste David cum sybylla,
Quantus tremor est futurus,
Quando Judex est venturus.

Krypton's hand was released from the door as soon as he had completed the saying. Krypton blinked several times to erase the blackness from his head. He first noticed that his hand was fine and second that the Door with No Handle had vanished. Ahead of Krypton was a long corridor; the Corridor of Balance.

Chapter Twelve

The hallway was tiled in squares of
black and white, but was only three tiles wide.
Krypton stepped onto the corridor's edge
and felt the atmosphere change dramatically.
Instead of thick, musty air, the air around him
was light with a mystical breeze flowing from
nowhere through the hallway. He looked down
and saw a black square directly in the middle of
two white tiles, the next set of tiles was a white
tile surrounded by two black tiles. The pattern
continued to alternate down the hall. Krypton
placed a foot squarely in the center of the nearest
black tile.

As soon as he put weight on down on the
tile, Krypton was engulfed in darkness. Hideous
screeching reached his ears, along with laughter;
the laughter of demons. Krypton covered his
ears in an attempt to block out the sound, but it
was too loud and seemed to be inside his very

head. It kept growing and growing. Krypton clenched his teeth and shut his eyes in pain. His knees soon gave out and Krypton went crashing onto the tiled floor.

The pain from falling overtook the pain from the screaming and laughing demons. Krypton took a few deep breaths and found that he had fallen out of the black tile and halfway on to the white one in front of it.

"Okay," he murmured, "black tiles are bad." Quickly, Krypton withdrew his feet and legs from the black square.

He stood and nursed his bruising elbow, careful to stay on the white tile. Out of nowhere, he became aware of flashes of bright white lights surrounding him. Hundreds of white glimmering lights danced around the light air. Krypton became transfixed on the marvel and stayed rooted to the spot. A small voice entered his ears.

"Sleep child… sleep." The voice was as clear and soft as the smallest bell in a cathedral. Krypton wanted to obey it, he had to obey it. His legs felt like gel beneath him; his eyes slowly closed as he began to sway.

Wait! shouted a voice in the back of his head, *You can't come this far for sleep!*

Krypton's eyes snapped open in realization. He understood. As he tried to move out of the white lights, everything turned black, just like when he had been on the black tile. Chaos erupted as again screeching noises and laughing demons pounded Krypton. It was as if his pain amused them. Before long his knees again failed to hold his weight, and Krypton toppled backwards.

Once again, as he hit the cold floor, the sounds came to a stop. Only the sound of a small ringing in his ears and the pounding of his heart remained. Krypton then realized why this place was called the Corridor of Balance. For, again, he had landed with half of his body on a black tile and the other half on white, but only a step away from where the Door with No Handle had once been.

The dark squares had to represent evil, death, and torture; this was bad from front to end. The white tiles, undoubtedly, stood for good, but as his elders had always taught him: too much of a good thing can become a bad thing. Hence the demons when Krypton attempted to escape. In order to be successful, a life must experience both good and bad. Although Krypton felt his life so far had been full of darkness, this was the time for him to be successful.

Krypton stood for the last time and wobbled a bit before placing one foot on a black square and the other on a white square. Peace, finally. His hypothesis had proved correct, so far. If he walked down the center and stepped on opposite squares each time, Krypton believed he could reach the end of this wretched hall.

Krypton stepped again, and felt nothing, it was still working. He took two more steps,

then a few more, still nothing. Soon he was on
a roll, left, right, left, right… *thud!* Krypton had
stepped into what felt like a wall. Now his face
hurt as much as the rest of his beaten body and
he stumbled backwards, taking care to still be
balanced. Krypton looked up to see what he had
run into. It looked like the corridor kept going
into a white mist that disappeared thousands
of paces in front of him. So Krypton placed his
hand out, trying to find what he had run into.

His hand disappeared. He pulled it back
quickly and examined it. It was fine and normal.
Was this a force field, or a doorway disguised
as an illusion to make the enterer think he still
had miles to walk, possibly making him retreat?
Krypton took a few deep breaths and stepped
through the doorway. It was like walking into a
frozen pond. When Krypton reached the other
side, he rubbed his arms to warm them before
rubbing his eyes. The sight before him took his
breath away.

Chapter Thirteen

The room Krypton had just entered made him feel like he was in a dream. Above him was a huge swirling mass of black and white, dark and light energy, with black being the dominate color. In front of Krypton was a narrow bridge suspended above an endless abyss. Beyond that were a few steps leading to another platform with a pedestal on it. Floating above the pedestal in mid-air was a greenish-black orb that seemed to be reflecting the attacking mass of energy above it. It seemed like the source of the chamber.

There was something else to the room that gave it the look of a dream. Everything looked... animated. Like the flat pictures Krypton would doodle in his text books. As he went to scratch his head, Krypton caught a glimpse of his hand and nearly jumped off the platform into the endless void below. He was an animation, too! His hand looked like a sketch, although he was not exactly two-dimensional. His coloring was flat, lacking in shadows and textures.

After a few moments, the panic inside him settled. The change would not harm him; he could still get through the force field he had left behind and would more than likely then be returned to a natural state. Krypton regained his strength and took a step toward the orb that he hoped would make him immortal.

His footsteps echoed through the otherwise silent chamber until he reached the first of the six stairs. A soft siren like sound met Krypton's ears; it was the sound of the colliding energy above him. Ascending the stairs, it grew louder, but not enough to annoy. When he reached the platform and saw the orb in front of him, a small burst of fear erupted in Krypton. The black energy flecked with white had been unmercifully attacking the orb even as Krypton drew nearer. It seemed too easy. All he had to do was place a hand over the orb and catch some of the energy. Krypton's animated fingers stretched out, but stopped halfway there; something inside him was hesitant.

Without intentionally meaning to do so, Krypton began thinking pessimistically. *I don't know what's going to happen. What if touching the energy kills me? I would fail and everything that I've done to get here would have been in vain.* Krypton's hand began to retreat from the orb.

I could stay on this world; I don't have to leave. I don't need excitement and adventure.

76

No, replied the same firm voice in Krypton's head from the Corridor of Balance, *you can't quit. What is dieing now?*

"Nothing," Krypton said aloud. Death was nothing now. Everyone, his family, Starchaser, they were afraid of death too, but it came to them in the end anyway.

"Why should we be afraid of something we cannot prevent? If death is what is in store for me here, then let me have it. I've been through enough to know that I am not afraid to die," Krypton finished aloud and firmly placed his hand over the orb. It felt like smooth warm glass.

Within an instant the energy above lashed at his hand instead of the orb. Krypton felt a huge surge of energy flowing through him, as he did not have the protection that the orb had. As it sped and channeled its way through his body, Krypton's vision swirled; his hand almost fell from its position on the orb. He squinted, straining his vision enough to see the orb begin to crack beneath his fingers. More energy came flooding now painfully into his body, causing immense agony to erupt in his shoulder blades.

The wailing sound of the energy mass screeched louder and louder, nearly drowning out the sounds of the crackling orb and Krypton's own screams. He grabbed the orb itself with two hands to prevent himself from being thrown backwards by the gust of air that pulsated down from the energy. Then, over the wailing, a thud met his ears and Krypton no longer felt the smooth orb beneath his burning palms. It had escaped his grasp with a sharp rocking motion and had fallen off the pedestal. Before he could discern in which direction the orb was rolling, Krypton was thrown backwards. His muscles tightened in preparation for a hard landing with ill effects. His head hit the sharp edge of a stair step and Krypton fell unconscious.

Chapter Fourteen

It was only a short while that he laid there on the steps. When he came to, Krypton had only a faint memory of what had happened. It was no longer freezing cold in the chamber, but comfortably warm. His head was throbbing along with his sore muscles. As he got to his feet, something soft brushed up against his still animated hand. Surprised, Krypton jumped and turned, expecting to see a strange creature behind him, seeking revenge for disrupting the orb, but he instead saw nothing but white... until his vision began to clear. Once it had set, Krypton found himself starring at a glimmering, white wing protruding from his shoulder blade.

Again he jumped, possibly higher, with surprise and alarm. To his right, he saw another wing, this one a jet black. Krypton looked back at the white wing. It was rimmed with bright fire that burned with what seemed the intensity

and darkness of the underworld. The black
wing fluttered and Krypton noticed the tip
where a golden halo dangled. No wonder there
had been pain in his shoulder blades.

"I have wings!" he exclaimed.

Still being animated, they looked a little
trite, but it was truly amazing all the same.
Krypton had become something like… a Demon
Angel. Perhaps it could be a name for a new race.

A glimmer directed his attention away
from the wings; the orb was rocking slowly at his
feet. Krypton scooped it up from the platform
before it got too far and stepped up the stairs
to place it back on its pedestal. There was a
small crack in the orb's side, but it did not seem
troublesome. Krypton felt strangely lighthearted
after it was safely nestled between its posts. He
had not a care in the world, nor did he worry
about what commotion his wings may bring to
public. There would be a way to walk crowded
streets again; he knew there had to be a way.

A loud thunderous roar brought Krypton
back to reality. There were now two masses
above him. One perfectly balanced with black
and white energy, the other pure black. It was
the black mass that was expanding, causing the
seemingly endless surroundings to suddenly
crack. Krypton leaped down the stairs and raced
across the bridge as fast as he could, pulling in
his wings to be more aerodynamic. He could
hear the energy behind him as he ran down the
Corridor of Balance, still careful to stay at peace

with the black and white tiles. Ahead was the faint outline of the Door with No Handle; it was materializing again!

Gritting his teeth and asking his legs for one last powerful drive, Krypton dove into the castle's hallway and the musty air. Krypton found himself rolling in the air and hitting the ground on his back at the base of his newly formed wings. He cringed then lay deathly still as the black energy swarmed out of the chamber and through the doorway just inches above his nose. Finally, the door completely solidified, and the hideous energy could no longer enter the real world.

Krypton appeared normal again, colored with textures instead of flat colors and the wings, his wings, looked even more amazing than they did in the chamber. Feathered with pure white and deep black, the colors of the fire and halo were stunning. Still admiring his new appendages, Krypton raised himself from the dusty floor just in time to feel the castle quake beneath him. The energy was trapped inside the castle walls and was threatening to leave, without using a door.

The Demon Angel broke into a run and turned a sharp corner into the stairwell, skipping down two steps at a time as the vibrations around him grew. Instead of heading straight and going out the secret entrance, Krypton turned left and found the front door. At the present moment, he was more afraid of the evil energy mass than the guards. It was right behind him again!

Halfway across the broken drawbridge, the sudden change in light caused Krypton to falter. It was already morning! He tumbled the rest of the way off of the bridge, just as the energy caused the castle walls to explode. Debris flanked Krypton, and he was forced to shield himself with his wings. Guards and peasants screamed; he could hear thumping footsteps all around him. The sound of the energy mass slowly melted into the surroundings. It had escaped the confining walls of Lonely Castle.

Finally, all was silent. At eight in the morning, when the streets are normally crowded with loud peasants, all was quiet. Krypton opened his eyes and lifted his wings to see the dust settling over a rubble-covered area where the castle had once been. The first thing Krypton noticed was the people of AnDev who had come to stare at him.

"Um... wow, wonder what happened?" Krypton muttered, attempting dully to make it seem as if he were innocent.

A sharp *click click* sounded behind the Demon Angel and drew his gaze to three guards with guns pointed in his direction.

No use compromising; they've already seen my wings.

Even though he was exhausted from the running he had already done across the marble floors of the once magnificent castle, Krypton was still somehow able to coax his legs away from the newfound danger. He dodged peasants who were shouting, "Demon!" and waving their pitchforks and shopping baskets as he sped along the dirt roads.

Krypton heard more shots and felt a sting of pain in his black wing. Krypton glanced towards the source, where a bloody hole was slowly closing in the flesh of his wing. A feather regenerated itself. Another shot rang out and Krypton felt pain shoot through his chest. He kept running. The bullet wound in his chest was healing too. He had been shot, but was healing! He really was invincible and immortal! Krypton ripped the bandage from his arm; that wound had already healed. It had worked!

With the angry mob still chasing him despite their ineffective bullets, Krypton turned another sharp corner and ran behind Sir Casente's house, diving into a large pile of hay. The mob ran out into the sparse forest beyond thinking they were still chasing after their demon. Krypton exhaled a long sigh of relief. All he had to do now was get to the teleportor in Sir Casente's kitchen cupboard and he would be free to travel other worlds.

Once the sound of shouting died down, Krypton crept out of the hay and folded his wings. The back window was dark, so Krypton had to assume that Sir Casente was not at home. He yanked open the door, almost taking it off its rusty hinges. Vividly, Krypton remembered the dark cabin, its kitchen and the wardrobe to his left leaning up against the wall.

He took a step toward the faintly glowing wardrobe, when an incredibly sharp strike on the back knocked Krypton to the ground. He landed on his hands and knees, but turned around in time to see Sir Casente standing over him with a frown on his face and one of the long metal pipes in his hands.

"Leave, Demon, and take your curses with you," he scowled, but then a sudden realization overtook his frown. "Wait, you're the boy from the newspaper. You weren't really writing an article, you were getting information for yourself!" he yelled in outrage.

"And you're extremely strong for your age," Krypton assured him rubbing the space between his shoulder blades. "I have a good reason for wanting to become immortal, just listen!"

"You were a demon before you became immortal!" Sir Casente continued, ignoring Krypton's pleading. "Unfortunately for you, I know how to kill those who cannot die!"

"Wait, stop!" Krypton tried to say, but was forced to back into the wardrobe as Sir Casente came closer, throwing down the pipe as he pulled a silver colored vial from his pocket. At the same time, the key to the wardrobe fell from his pocket onto the floor. Sir Casente stooped to pick it up and placed it on the table beside him.

"I shall finish you as you finished my ancestors' pride! My pride! This vial will trap you; crush you, until your soul collapses!"

"No wait, listen!"

As Krypton held up his hands to try and hold Sir Casente and the silver vial back, a strange white light was emitted from his palms, blasting Sir Casente back and to the ground with an "*Oof!*"

When the light vanished, Krypton clumsily got to his feet and looked at his glowing palms. "Whoa... cool! I've never been able to do that before!" He tried to do the trick again, but nothing happened, even after his palms had stopped glowing. "Perhaps it only works when I'm in trouble."

Krypton spotted Sir Casente motionless on the ground before him. He quickly checked for a pulse. The old man was only unconscious and would not get to give Krypton a preview of how Atherialism actually worked. Then his gaze met the black key Sir Casente had placed on the table. Krypton quickly grabbed it and stepped over the remaining fallen pipes to the oak wardrobe.

The click of the lock opening matched a skip in his heartbeat; Krypton was ready to start a new life. His dreams would lead him where he felt he was supposed to be. Krypton lifted the green circle from the shelf, set it on the ground, and flipped the box shaped switch on the side to turn on the machine. The teleportor emitted an even brighter green glow before Krypton stepped onto it and was swallowed by the warm lime-light that would take him to a forever home or would continue his adventure in another world.

Printed in the United States
128485LV00001B/447/P